MW01042789

Don't Talk to Strangers

To Luca — The coolest little guy in the whole world. I love you 7,061,997 times. — Kevi

This book is dedicated to David J. Passalacqua — our teacher, friend, and inspiration. — JibJab

ISBN 0-439-31385-6

Text and illustrations copyright © 2003 by ONE GAZILLION, INC.

All rights reserved.   Published by Scholastic Inc., 557 Broadway, New York, NY 10012.
SCHOLASTIC, CARTWHEEL BOOKS, and associated logos are trademarks and/or registered trademarks of Scholastic Inc.
ROLLERBLADES is a trademark of Benetton Sportsystem. Used without permission.

Library of Congress Cataloging-in-Publication Data available

The text type was set in Compacta Bold.
Book design by Steven Scott.

12 11 10 9 8 7 6 5 4 3 2 1   03 04 05 06 07

Printed in China   62
First Scholastic printing, February 2003

Don't Talk to Strangers

By Kevi
Illustrated by JibJab Media

SCHOLASTIC INC.

New York   Toronto   London   Auckland   Sydney   Mexico City   New Delhi   Hong Kong   Buenos Aires

It might be that lady with the crazy hat,
the real cool dude with the kitty cat.

The man with the van from the grocery place,
the lady with the baby with the silly face.

You'll never know if a stranger's good or bad.
You'll never know if a stranger's happy or mad.

You'll never really know if a stranger's cool,
so always try to stick to Kevi's simple rules.

Don't talk to strangers in the park.
Never talk to strangers in a car.

Stay away from strangers after school.
Don't talk to strangers—that's the rule!

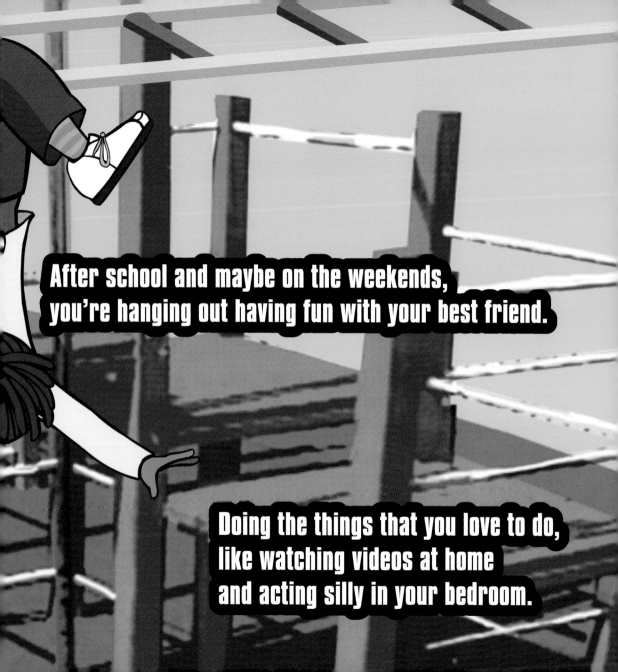

After school and maybe on the weekends, you're hanging out having fun with your best friend.

Doing the things that you love to do, like watching videos at home and acting silly in your bedroom.

Your dad's at work, and your mom's across the street, talking to Betty, her best friend with the big feet.

You don't mind 'cause the front door's locked,
and Betty's number's by the phone, right by the clock.

All of a sudden you hear the doorbell ring.
It's not your mom or dad—they have keys to get in.

Sometimes strangers might knock on your door, but never open up the door unless you're positive sure.

Just play it safe, and pick up the phone.
Tell your mom or dad what's going on and to hurry home.

'Cause you never really know if a stranger's cool,
so always try to stick to Kevi's simple rules.

Riding your skateboard down at the beach, or Rollerblading on a nearby street.

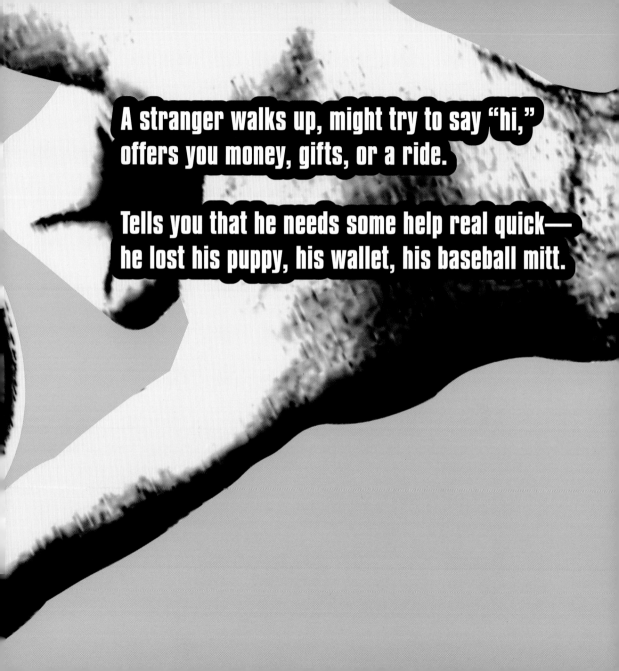

A stranger walks up, might try to say "hi,"
offers you money, gifts, or a ride.

Tells you that he needs some help real quick—
he lost his puppy, his wallet, his baseball mitt.

And if you're never sure just what to do, always try to stick to Kevi's simple rules.

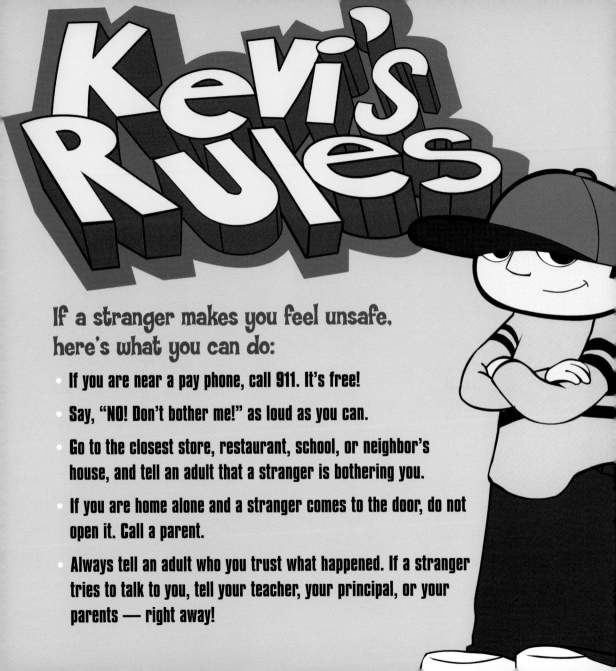

Kevi's Rules

If a stranger makes you feel unsafe, here's what you can do:

- If you are near a pay phone, call 911. It's free!

- Say, "NO! Don't bother me!" as loud as you can.

- Go to the closest store, restaurant, school, or neighbor's house, and tell an adult that a stranger is bothering you.

- If you are home alone and a stranger comes to the door, do not open it. Call a parent.

- Always tell an adult who you trust what happened. If a stranger tries to talk to you, tell your teacher, your principal, or your parents — right away!